The Canterpurry Tales

Also by Stanley Salmons

ALEXEI'S TREE AND OTHER STORIES

A BIT OF IRISH MIST

THE TOMB

FOOTPRINTS IN THE ASH

NH_3

THE MAN IN TWO BODIES

THE DOMINO MAN

COUNTERFEIT

The Canterpurry Tales

Stanley Salmons

Illustrated by
Martin Preston.

ISBN: 1542397235

ISBN-13: 978-1542397230

This novel is a work of fiction. Any resemblance to actual animals,
living or dead, is entirely coincidental

Stanley Salmons was born in Clapton, East London. He is internationally known for his work in the fields of biomedical engineering and muscle physiology, published in over two hundred scientific articles and twelve scientific books. He can draw from this broad scientific experience in his parallel existence as a fiction writer. More than forty short stories and five other novels have been published, but this is his first full-length children's story.

STANLEY SALMONS

For my grandchildren
Josh, Emmie, Skye, Harry, Jamie, Bella
Bobby and Alec

Chapter 1

Bummus McBaggus

The ambush was ready. The three were well concealed behind a clump of gorse. By moving their heads from side to side to peer between the branches they could watch their target labour slowly up the hillside. The small figure moved in and out of view behind the purple bursts of heather and the yellow pea-flowers of the gorse. At one point it disappeared for minutes on end, hidden by an outcrop of lichen-covered rocks. Then it reappeared, still coming on.

They watched, and they waited.

Behind the gorse the tails of the three assailants extended along the ground, one black, one tabby, and one ginger striped with white. The tips twitched in anticipation. Three pairs of haunches wiggled to get the best possible toehold on the dusty ground; three pairs of ears turned forward, alert for the slightest sound.

The owner of the black tail murmured, "When he gets to that rock, I'm going to spring out and crumbusticate him."

"And I'll croddle his ears," said Molly, the tabby kitten.

"What shall I do, Crustum?" asked Flumbo. He was the ginger and white. He was slower than the others because of a tummy that spread a little on either side as he crouched on the ground. Flumbo was always keen to join in any game even if he didn't quite understand what was going on.

"You can scrunge his tail," came the reply.

"There'll be no crumbusticating, croddling, or scrunging while I'm around, Crustum McBustum," came a strong Yorkshire voice from behind them.

The three kittens ducked their heads, looked slowly round, and drooped.

"We were only playing, Mrs Tibbs," Crustum mewdled to the large tabby who was towering over them. He gave his white bib a quick lick to cover the awkwardness of the moment.

"You should be ashamed of yourselves," she said sternly. "Can't you see the poor thing is all in?"

They looked again, and as they did so the figure stopped, swayed, and collapsed onto its side.

Mrs Tibbs set off briskly towards it and the three kittens followed.

Crustum managed to catch up.

"Are you sure it's safe, Mrs Tibbs? I mean, he could be lying like that so he can use all four paws, couldn't he?"

Mrs Tibbs glanced at him with approval.

"You're right to be cautious, Crustum. But I think I know what an exhausted creature looks like, and believe you me, this is one."

They hung back as Mrs Tibbs approached the animal, sniffed him over, then picked him up in her strong jaws by the scruff of the neck.

"Is he dead?" Crustum enquired with interest.

This time Mrs Tibbs didn't respond – indeed she could hardly do so with her mouth fully occupied. The newcomer dangled limply, like a doll, and swung from side to side as she turned and made her way back up the slope, front legs straddled.

Crustum nodded confidently to the others. "I think he is."

"Eeu-urgh," said Molly. "I don't like dead things."

"You like them well enough when they're for dinner."

"That's different. I mean I don't like dead moggies."

"Have you ever seen a dead moggy?"

"No."

"Then how do you know you don't like them?"

"Oh shut up, Crustum!"

She lolloped away in pursuit of the retreating figure of Mrs Tibbs. Crustum shrugged and followed suit.

"Wait for me!"

They paused and looked round at Flumbo, who'd

stopped, breathing hard.

"Come on, Flumbo!"

"It's… very… steep," said Flumbo. He took some deep breaths and recovered sufficiently to join Crustum. Then they walked slowly up to Molly. "It's all right for you two," he panted. "I'm bigger boned."

"Is that what you call it?" said Molly, with a sardonic lift of her side whiskers.

By the time the three had arrived back at the cave there was quite a crowd around Mrs Tibbs and the new arrival.

Molly was the smallest kitten, and she managed to worm her way through the forest of legs to the front. Soon she came back to pass on the latest developments.

"He's opened his eyes and he's taken a little water," she said breathlessly. "And he ate some trout Mrs Tibbs gave him."

Flumbo's eyes opened wide in dismay. "She gave him our trout?!"

"It's not *your* trout, Flumbo. Flashpad McGraw caught it. And Mrs Tibbs said the poor thing's starving. You can see his ribs. His pads are bleeding – he must have walked for miles and miles. She said we had to be generous."

"I suppose so," Flumbo complained, "Only I was looking forward to that trout."

One onlooker detached himself from the crowd and

walked slowly past them. It was Gloomie McDoom, a long-haired tabby with white hair all over his chin and

very bushy black eye-whiskers.

"Another mouth to feed," he sighed as he came past. "Where's it all going to end, I ask m'self?"

There was plenty of daylight left to play outside. When the sun started to go down, the three kittens went back into the cave to stare at the newcomer. He had revived a little and was sitting in a sphinx-like pose, paws stretched out in front of him. He seemed to be mainly black, although he had white mittens and there was more white underneath, spreading up onto both chops. His side whiskers and eye whiskers were very long; some were black and some were white. He looked up at them, his eyes round and golden.

"How did I get here?" he asked.

"She brought you," said Crustum, nodding in the direction of the large tabby, who was not far away. Hearing this she rose, stretched her front legs, unsheathed and sheathed her claws, and strolled over.

"Thank you very much, Miss, er…"

She spoke with slow emphasis.

"They call me *Mrs* Tibbs."

"Well," he said. "Thank you very much, Mrs Tibbs."

"Where did you come from, love?" she asked.

"London."

Her chops folded kindly. "If you're feeling up to it," she said, "would you like to tell us what 'appened to yer?"

Some of the others drew closer so that they could hear.

"Oh, it's the usual thing, I suppose. The water kept rising and it started to come into the house. My people were getting their stuff together, ready to move. There was some talk about going to higher ground further north. Then they started to argue because woman-pet wanted to take me, and man-pet said it was impossible. I didn't wait to find out. I kept to the roofs and managed to hop on a lorry pointing north. It ended up in Glasgow."

"How did you hear about us?" Crustum asked.

"A puss I met in a wool shop said she'd heard there was a community living in a cave up here. I set off the following day. It was much further than I thought. Still, once you've started you can't really turn back, can you? It was very tiring, especially the soft, hummocky bit down there, just before the hill."

"That'd be th' peat bog," supplied Mrs Tibbs.

"Makes a real mess of your paws," Flumbo said. "Take ages to lick clean afterwards."

"Then there was the hill, and in the end I just couldn't take another step." He looked at Mrs Tibbs. "That's when you must have found me."

Molly said, "That's not a very interesting story."

"Molly!" Mrs Tibbs exclaimed.

"Well, it isn't."

The newcomer hung his head.

"I suppose I'm not a very interesting moggy. Never have been, really."

"What's your name?" Molly demanded.

"I don't know. Man-pet called me all sorts of things."

He looked around at his small audience. "You know the way humans have a habit of getting their legs tangled up with you?"

The older ones nodded vigorously.

"Well, man-pet used to call me a lot of names when that happened. Too many to remember. I think one was 'A great streak of—'"

Mrs Tibbs interrupted firmly. "Thank you, I don't think we need to 'ear details. What did woman-pet call you?"

"'Liquorice'."

"Liquorice?" exclaimed Crustum. "What kind of a name is that?"

"Well, I think it's because I'm black on top and white underneath." He sat up properly and lifted a paw to show them the snowy white fur that went the length of his tummy. "They said I reminded them of something called Allsorts."

"What are Allsorts?" asked Flumbo, who guessed it might be something to eat.

"Something they suck to rot their teeth, I believe."

Gladys Morningbags, a plump ginger-and-white, spoke up. "One of my little humans used to eat them. Made her lips all black."

Crustum wrinkled his nose and said, "Ooergh!"

Pete Gumbo bristled and half rose.

"And what be wrong with black lips?" he

9

challenged, drawing his chops back over lips and gums that were very black indeed.

"Er, nothing, Pete," Crustum said hastily. "On a mog they look great. On a human, not so good."

Pete subsided.

"Well, I think 'Liquorice' is a dopey name for a little bumbag like you," Molly sniffed.

"That's it!" said Crustum. "We'll call him Bummus McBaggus!" He turned to their new friend. "What do you think of that?"

"Bummus McBaggus?" He tilted his head to one side, then the other, then smiled. "Why not?"

Chapter 2

Count Gropius's tale

Bit by bit Bummus began to regain his strength. There was plenty of food, for a lot of the day was spent hunting on the moor, and when the others came back there was always something left over for him. The dust of his long journey fell away, and he even managed to lick a bit of a shine into his coat.

The kittens – Crustum, Molly, and Flumbo – were quite curious about their new acquaintance, and they often sat with him during the day.

"Do you have a mother?" Flumbo asked, a wistful expression on his face.

"I don't think so."

"Everyone has a mother, silly," Molly said.

"Well, all I'm saying is I don't remember having one. My people-pets said I was a 'rescue cat' – whatever that means."

"It means you rescued them," Molly said confidently.

"Oh." He nodded, then asked, "Do you have a mother?"

Flumbo started to say, "We did have one but she was—"

Crustum and Molly turned sharply on him and his ears drooped. "Sorry. I mean… I miss her, that's all."

Bummus looked from one to the other. A needling sensation from his survival instinct told him something was wrong, but he would have to leave it for the moment.

Crustum looked towards the entrance. "The others are going hunting."

"We'd like to go with, but they won't let us," Molly said. "We're too small."

"I'd like to go, too," Bummus said, "but I have my job to do."

As the newest arrival it fell to him to look after the fire. It was a simple affair, just a pile of crackling twigs on the floor a little way inside the entrance, with a ring of stones to keep it small. He didn't know how it had got there, but he was told that on no account must it be allowed to go out. So each day, rain or shine, he'd have to go out on the moor to fetch more fuel. There was no lack of it, and if it was wet he would bring it inside to dry out. It was a wearisome job, and the old gorse branches and dried-up clumps of heather pricked his mouth. Still, it had its compensations. On a wet and windy day it was nice to stretch out next to it after he'd fetched in a good pile. When the light faded the others would come in and spend a happy hour or two with the catches, pulling feathers, turning their heads to chew bone and gristle, and choking up fur balls. Then they came near to the fire to go to sleep. At that point, of course, he had to relinquish his place. He'd settle down not far away, and the twins would curl up nearby.

It was a comfortable enough routine but something about it made him feel uneasy. He'd always found the best time for mousing was at night. Why didn't anyone here go out after dark?

After a few days he decided to explore the cave. It was nice and dry and very deep with many unexpected recesses. As some cats stayed there when the others went out he never knew what would be around the next corner. That was how he came to meet Count Gropius.

"I hear you come from Eng-land, darling."

The voice sailed down from the wall on his right. He approached the source. As his eyes adjusted to the darkness a ledge took shape, and on it a great mound of pure white fur. The fur then separated into an ear, which was moving rhythmically back and forth, and a paw which, his ears told him, was being licked with a similar rhythm. When the head finally turned and the face appeared, Bummus saw that it was a large Silver Persian, with a flattened muzzle that almost disappeared under a deeply wrinkled brow. The eyes were an alarming green.

"How fascinating for you!" the voice continued

mildly. The tone was at odds with the facial expression, which was fixed in a disdainful scowl. "Tell me, are they frightfully primitive down there?"

"Well, I wouldn't say…" Bummus ventured, before he realized that an answer was not expected.

"I am Count Gropius Crudnitz. I come from Liechtenstein, you know."

He gave one front paw a final lick with a very pink tongue. "Ah, it was such a cultured society I lived in. This is a rough and crude existence for someone like me, but I suppose it has its compensations. If I think very hard I might even think of one." He snirtled. Then, with a baleful look at Bummus, he added, "Harrumph, that was a little joke."

A very little one, Bummus thought. The Count now seemed reluctant to continue so he asked a question.

"How did you come to be here?"

The Persian sighed. "When the rivers rose in Europe, everyone – simply everyone – took to the mountains. Being located in the Alps our tiny country filled up with people. Absolute riff-raff, my dear – positive cavemen, some of them. It became very crowded and food ran short. They were fighting each other for scraps, darling – scraps, imagine that! Then they started to look at me in a very funny way and I decided it was time to leave." He sighed again. "I'm sure you aren't interested in all this."

"But I am. Please go on."

"Oh," the Count said, brightening a little. "Well, all right, then. You see, the woman-pet in my charge had decided she wasn't going to leave. 'Nothing and no one will induce me to move from here,' she said – her very words. Well, if she was determined to stay, how was I to get out of there? Fortunately, my dear, I come from a long line of highly intelligent pussycats." He drew himself up. "It may interest you to know that I am a direct descendant of His Imperial Pussiness, Crumbustian the Seventh. My illustrious ancestor spent his entire life being carried around on a cushion."

Bummus made a "fancy-that?" sort of noise in his throat.

"Woman-pet had a friend who was more sensible," he continued. "This friend had already decided to go. I slipped into her house while she was packing. She was stuffing her furs into a suitcase. Every sort of fur – mink, squirrel, ocelot, seal. One felt quite sorry for the poor creatures – well, perhaps not the mink, but the others. There wasn't room in the suitcase so she put some in her hand baggage and I got in while her back was turned. It was a bit stuffy in there but very comfortable. Fur's lovely for sleeping. Made me feel like I was a little kitty again, snuggled up with Mummy and my brothers and sisters."

Bummus's attention drifted. He was wondering what it would have been like to have brothers and sisters when he was small, all curled up together in a warm, furry bundle. It sounded lovely.

The Count didn't seem to have noticed the faraway look in his eyes. He continued without a pause.

"I was bumped around a bit but I slept for most of the journey. Unfortunately there was nothing to eat. I tried chewing some of the furs but they were very hard and dry. Someone of my pedigree is simply not accustomed to being hungry. When we reached our destination and she unpacked I was glad to jump out. It gave her a bit of a shock, I dare say, but she did over-react. You should have heard her, the drama queen! Quite lacking in refinement, I thought. She opened the door to scream for help and I took the breeze, as I believe my American cousins put it."

"And where was this?" Bummus asked, out of politeness. The Count was so full of himself that it was hard to maintain more than a mild interest.

"In a hotel in Edinburgh, as it turned out. I could smell food, so I went downstairs and found the kitchen. One of the staff tossed a bit of skin and gristle my way. Skin and gristle, darling! I looked meaningfully at the leg of chicken in his hand but he didn't take the hint. Then a waitress came along. She, at least, saw what I was and – yes?" he snapped suddenly.

Crustum was standing there, shifting from one paw to the other. Bummus could barely hide his relief at the interruption.

"Please sir, Mrs Tibbs sent me. They're just going out to look for nesting curlew and she asks if you'd like to join them."

"Like…? No, I do not like! Count Gropius Crudnitz does not like to drag himself across miles of thorny moorland looking for eggs or curlews."

"Sir," Crustum said, his voice barely audible, "She says if you want to eat, you have to hunt."

The Count rose to his paws. His back continued to rise until it formed a great spiky arch, then settled down again.

"This just illustrates the problem," he said petulantly. "Mrs Tibbs – a common moggy – now tells me what to do! You see, what's-your-name—?"

"Bummus, sir."

"You see, Bummus – what a strange name – society has gone quite, quite mad. Civilization has collapsed! There's no longer any respect for the upper classes. I remember my cousin, the Grand Duke Schnittke-Gezubble, saying—"

Crustum cleared his throat.

"Excuse me, sir, but does that mean you're not coming?"

"Doh! Yes, I'm coming. Under protest, you understand? Under protest. I want to make that quite clear."

And he jumped neatly down and swaggered off towards the entrance.

Crustum winked at Bummus.

"A real windbag, isn't he?"

"Does he ever catch anything?"

Crustum shook his head. "With that coat they can spot him a mile off. He'll get the occasional bird or mouse if he hides behind something and surprises it. It makes his day. Don't let him hear you say it, but under all that fur he's just an alley cat."

Chapter 3

Septimus Dufax's tale

Crustum, Molly, and Flumbo were now more or less constant companions to Bummus. If the weather turned nasty, as it often did, they'd come back into the cave and keep him company. Then they'd sit together by the fire and talk about what had been going on outside. The little ones didn't care for worms, they said, and butterflies and moths made their mouths feel funny, but spiders and grasshoppers were nice and crunchy. Flumbo had once tried to eat a toad, and he'd looked so comical with froth all round his mouth that Crustum and Molly had rolled around in the heather, laughing until their ribs ached. Occasionally one of them would catch a mouse or shrew, and then they had to take it back to show the others. It seemed that finds like this had an odd way of disappearing suddenly, and they'd be lucky if they ever got to eat them. The larger cats, like Mrs Tibbs and Pete Gumbo, would catch rabbits and squirrels and birds such as meadow pipits and black partridge. But everyone agreed that the finest hunter of them all was Sir Baddersley Pike. Bummus was curious to meet him, but he was out on one of his long hunts and would probably be gone for days.

During these conversations it emerged that if he wanted to know anything – anything at all – the one to ask was Septimus Dufax. Bummus decided to pay him a visit and the kittens tagged along.

Septimus was a rather thin, grey-and-white cat, very

pale around the muzzle, but his amber eyes were as large and wise as an owl's.

On this occasion there were two other elderly cats with him. They moved round to make room and introduced themselves as Smellysox McBride and Crompton Gristleback. Smellysox was a tabby with black paws, and Crompton was a sort of gunmetal colour, although his coat looked rather patchy and thin.

Bummus said politely, "Pleased to meet you. I'm Liquor—er, I'm Bummus McBaggus. I'm the new arrival. This is a very nice cave you have here."

"We're fortunate, aren't we?" said Smellysox. "It was occupied by a human when we first came. There were only a few of us then. I think the human enjoyed a bit of company because he used to throw us scraps. He was terribly dirty, but then humans never lick themselves, do they?"

"No," Bummus agreed. "At least, not that I've ever seen."

The conversation had evidently reminded Smellysox that something required attention, and he shot a front paw and gave it some long licks inside, right from the elbow. Crompton took up the story.

"It's a big cave, so there was room for all of us. Then one day the man went out and didn't come back. We never found out what happened to him. He left a few things behind, human things: a couple of pots, a blanket, that big sheet of polythene over there. We found some animal bones, too, of a type I've never seen. I think there must have been humans living here for years and years. Of course the really important thing he left us was the fire."

"I was wondering where that came from."

Smellysox had finished his wash, and now resumed the conversation. "It makes all the difference, that fire. It keeps us warm and safe, especially in the winter. We never let it go out or we'd never be able to light it again. Someone always has to look after it."

And right now that someone is me, Bummus thought. But there was still much he wanted to know.

"I haven't seen any humans up here," he said. "Even in Glasgow there was hardly anyone around. Where have they all gone?"

Smellysox and Crompton both looked at Septimus, who turned his large eyes on Bummus.

"It was the sewers." He had a thin voice, but it carried wisdom and authority.

"The sewers?"

"Yes. Have you heard of global warming?"

Bummus said, "Er, yes, but I'm a bit vague about..."

"Well, the ice at the top and bottom of the world melted, which made the sea rise and come into the towns. The sewers couldn't handle that much water, so all the smelly stuff overflowed into the streets. After a while the humans started to fall sick and die. Cholera, typhoid, and dysentery. Worse in combination than the plagues of the Middle Ages."

"Where did you learn all those big words, Mr Dufax?" asked Molly.

Septimus gave a whisker a careful scrood before

answering. "My human-pets used to leave their computer on overnight. I would surf the net while they were asleep."

"So you can read?" Molly said. "Gosh, you must be ever, ever so clever."

"It's not so hard. Of course I could only understand the pictures at first. But after a while – look, little one, can you tell the difference between the pawprints left by a mouse and a partridge?"

"Of course," she replied instantly.

"And between a partridge and a moorhen?"

"Yes."

"Well, there you are. It's called pattern recognition, and it applies to words as well as pictures. They never knew what I was doing, of course. Nice people – you know, quite manageable. Didn't see a lot of him; used to be off on what he called business trips. She was usually around, though. Had a nice warm, comfortable lap, my woman-pet." He sighed.

"I bet she used to do the stroking and tickling-round-the ears-and-chin bit, though," Smellysox said.

Septimus nodded sadly, and Crompton said, "We all had to put up with that."

"I didn't mind really," Smellysox said. "I mean, you close your eyes and give them a bit of a purr, and if it makes them happy, what's the difference?"

"Are yours dead now?"

"I expect so."

"Mine are."

"Mine, too."

"Are they all dead, Mr Dufax? All the humans, I mean," asked Crustum.

"Good heavens, no. Maybe in the cities they are. Most big cities grew up next to rivers – the rivers were the highways before anyone built roads, y'see. So when the sea level rose they were the first to go. But there were other humans living at higher altitudes, like we're doing here. Of course, they don't dare to venture down into the lower levels now in case they catch the diseases."

"I see," said Bummus. "So there are just a few humans left, stuck in little pockets here and there? What about cats like us?"

"I'm sure they've had the good sense to find safe places, just as we did."

"Well, thank you very much," Bummus said, rising to his paws. "This has been really interesting."

Septimus gave him an indulgent smile. "Any time, young Bummus. Take care, now."

As Bummus left with the kittens Pete Gumbo appeared at the entrance and strolled over. The kittens backed off a little as Pete gave Bummus a greeting nudge with his shoulder.

"Hi man, how goes it? Someone said you came up

from the old smoke – London. Come over 'ere. Let's have a word."

Chapter 4

Pete Prawn Gumbo's tale

Pete Gumbo was a long-limbed, well-muscled cat, black from the tip of his nose to the tip of his tail, and on his head he wore a small baseball cap backwards. He led Bummus a short distance from the entrance and paused to gnash urgently at an imaginary tangle. As he did so Bummus looked round and noticed that the kittens had gone. Pete straightened up.

"So, you're from London? Me too. Brixton. How about you?"

"Hendon," Bummus replied.

"Don't know nuffin' about Hendon. Off my territory – know what I mean? Posh, is it?"

"I suppose you could say so."

"Oo-ee, listen to the brother talk! I should think it is posh up there! Well, I tell ya, mate, there was nuffin' fancy in my part of the world. I lived on the streets."

"Who fed you?"

"Who? Everyone! I just toured the takeaways. It's all a question of timing, see? You go down there of an evening and have a nose around. People buy meals and chuck 'em away half finished. You get a lot of choice: Chinese, Indian, Thai." He scrooded a whisker.

"Now me, I have a fondness for Cajun. Very tasty, Cajun. That's why they call me Pete Prawn Gumbo, see? Very partial to gumbo, I am."

"I thought humans used dustbins."

"Hark at him! Wheelies, you mean! Never. Not where I lived. They chucked the stuff on the street. Wheelies are useless – except for dumping dead bodies in. Ya-ha, ya-ha!"

Bummus smiled politely. When the gales of laughter had died down, he asked:

"Did you walk here, too?"

"Eh? Me walk? You must be joking, man! Hitched a ride on a train, I did. Train was packed but plenty of room in the mail van. Found a mouse in there, too. Quite nice, but I prefer gumbo. Jumped a four-by-four after that and got off when the smell told me there were brothers around. So, whaddaya think of it up here?"

"It seems very nice. And it's good to be back on the ground. In London I had to travel over roofs and along fences to keep my paws dry."

"Oh yeah, know what ya mean. Gets pretty wet here too, mind. Does it rain? Does it ever! Comes down in men, women, and children." He flashed a sideways glance at Bummus. "Like that, do you? The humans say 'It's raining cats and dogs', so I say 'It's raining men, women, and children'. All right, eh?"

"Mmm," Bummus agreed enthusiastically. "Very good."

"Mind you," Pete continued, "fishing's good in the rain."

"Oh, do you go fishing?"

"Me? Hell, no. Haven't a clue. Flashpad McGraw's the one for fishing. Met him, have you?" He didn't wait for an answer. "Dab hand, old Flash. Comes back with a fish nine times out of ten. Doesn't mind the rain, either. Sits by the fire after, to dry out. Like trout, do you?"

"Yes, very much."

"Yeah, not bad at all. Not as good as gumbo but very

passable, very passable indeed. Can you fish?"

"I don't know, I've never tried."

"Never tried? Ha, you're a careful one, ain't ya? Maybe you should get old Flash to show you some time."

"I'd like that. But I don't think I'd like to do it in the rain. It rained a bit this morning when I was gathering stuff for the fire. Not heavily – more like a mist – but it sort of sticks to your fur in little globs."

"Yeah, you get a lot of that here." Pete's manner seemed to have changed. He looked around, then dropped his voice and leaned towards Bummus's ear. "Listen, friend: if one of those mists comes down when you're out on the moor, keep your wits about you – know what I'm saying? Eyes peeled and ears – what do you do with ears, anyway? You can't peel 'em."

"Er, I've no idea. Keep them moving?"

"Yeah, whatever. Best to be back in the cave when it's like that." He brightened up again. "Safe an' dry, with the fire and everythin'. No problem with that. Why get wet? I say. Not worth it, not even for trout. Here, where did your mates go?"

Bummus winced. "I think maybe they went back to see their mother."

A shadow seemed to pass across Pete's face. "Nah. Mummy's not with us any more, know what I mean?"

"Oh, how sad. What happened?"

He looked away, suddenly evasive. "One of those things, innit? Crustum and Molly are twins. Flumbo joined them when his Mum... yes, well, he don't have no Mum, neither, so they hang out together. Talking of twins, look who's here! Hallo, Lady P! How are we today, then, my darling?"

Pete was addressing a slim Sable Burmese who was passing by with two kittens, one brown, one grey.

She nodded graciously. "Hallo, Peter," she said. "We are all extremely well, thank you." Then, to the twins, "Now don't primp, kittens, walk nicely."

Pete looked at Bummus, rocked his head from side to side and formed his lips carefully. "We are extremely well, we are," he said, in a quiet imitation of the refined reply. "Ya-ha. There's real aristocracy for you."

"Nice kittens," Bummus ventured.

"Yeah, growing up fast, they are, the young'uns. They'll soon be out hunting with us. McPee and McPoo, I call them." Bummus realized his astonishment must have shown, because Pete added hastily, "Not their *real* names, brother! The little girl's Poppy, and the little boy's Mungo. Daddy is Sir Baddersley Pike. He's the big honcho round here. He's off huntin' right now. You'll meet him when he gets back."

But something Pete had said was still troubling Bummus. "Pete, what happened to Crustum's mother. And Flumbo's?"

Pete's whiskers twitched. "Ah, you don't wanna know stuff like that." He rubbed a paw over his stomach. "Well, I'm feeling a bit peckish. Let's see what the weather's doing to us outside."

As they walked back towards the entrance Bummus was still uneasy. Crustum and Molly had stopped Flumbo from saying what happened to his mother. Pete seemed to know but he didn't want to say anything either. What was it? Pete had warned him about being out in the mist, and no one here went out after dark. There was something they weren't telling him, something important.

His attention was distracted as they passed a recess on one side of the cave. Tucked comfortably into it was a curvaceous white Ragdoll with a diamond collar. She was totally absorbed, painting her claws with a bright red berry.

"Who's that?" Bummus asked Pete.

"That? That's Dolly Sparkle," he said. "Chic chick. Go on. Give her a hallo. I'm going to find myself someone to eat."

As Bummus turned towards the recess, Pete added over his shoulder, "Word of advice, brother. Whatever you do, don't get her singing."

Bummus started to ask why, but Pete had already skipped out of the entrance and into the sunshine.

Chapter 5

Dolly Sparkle's tale

Bummus took a few steps, but then he felt the blood rush to his face and he hesitated about going any nearer. Up to now it had never bothered him that he was a plain old black-and-white moggy, but faced with a creature of such obvious pedigree he felt distinctly inferior.

Dolly finished the second front paw, retracted the claws, and skilfully licked off the berry juice that had spread onto her pure white socks. Then she lifted a paw and extended the claws, apparently admiring the colour. At this point she seemed to register his presence and slowly turned her gaze in his direction. He was transfixed by a pair of huge blue eyes.

"Well, are y'all comin' in or are you jus' goin' to stand there?" she called.

Bummus took a few steps forward, burning with embarrassment.

"I'm sorry, I didn't mean to stare. It's just that... you're ever so pretty."

"Why, what a perfectly sweet thing for y'all to say. What's your name?"

"Erm, Bummus McBaggus."

"We...ell, with a name like that, y'all must come from the Highlands of Scotland."

The way she said it, it came out like "Higherlands of Scotterland".

"Er, no. Hendon, actually."

"But your name is jus' wonderful..."

"The others gave it to me." Then, thinking of the sound track of films he'd heard on television while he was stretched in front of the fire back at home, he plucked up courage and asked, "Are you from America?"

"The States? Me? Why, no. I guess y'all are thinking 'bout my accent. I got that from my lady-pet. She was a real fine Country singer." She stroked the back of her head delicately with a front paw. "I have a most refined ear for music, so I couldn't help but end up speakin' like that myself."

"Did you go to her concerts?"

He found her eyes on him again. It sent a tingle through his pawpads.

"I mos' surely did. She would never dream of steppin' out of the house without me. Mos' times I would curl up in her dressing room, and I'd be there when she came back for the interval, and there again when it was all over. She would get the Stage Manager to bring me somethin' to eat. Some o' them didn't mind. Some hated it, but they were obliged to." She sighed.

"She was a star, you see. So I was, too."

"How wonderful," Bummus murmured.

"Yes. I sure do miss her."

"How did you, er, become separated?"

She heaved another sigh, the snowy fur on her chest standing out in a way that made Bummus feel even more funny inside. "We-all were in Selkirk, on tour," she said. "It had been rainin' for days and days. Then someone said a river had broke its banks. It came into the theatre, cascadin' down the steps like a waterfall, and the people were all shoutin' and cryin'! Lady-pet picked me up and ran outside. The water was runnin' fast along the street and it was very deep. I saw some rubber dingies comin' and my lady-pet tried to wade out to them."

Bummus was alarmed to see a large tear form in one of those big blue eyes.

"I jus' knew she'd never make it." The tear welled and spilt down a furry cheek. She wiped it away with the back of a paw. "I saw a front door floatin' past and I struggled out of her arms and jumped onto it. She called out my name – Dolly! That was the very las' time I saw her."

"I'm so sorry," Bummus said. He allowed a respectful moment of silence to pass before continuing. "Selkirk must be a long way from here, though."

"I guess. You know, I was ridin' this door for simply ages and ages and then it jammed into a fence and got stuck. I jumped off and walked along the fence for a bit. I never did have to walk that much before and I got pretty darned tired, y'know. It was still rainin' and my fur was so wet I must have looked a fright! Then I saw a man loadin' sheep onto a trailer. I hopped in and got on the back of one. I'm quite delicate," she added, patting the back of her head again. "I don't think that stupid woolly had any idea I was there."

"But you didn't know where they were going?"

"No, darlin', I jus' wanted out of there. I don't know how far we drove. I fell asleep." She looked at Bummus, eyes wide. "I was totally grief-stricken for my lady-pet, of course, but my little body was quite worn out. I jus' could not help myself."

"Of course," Bummus said reassuringly. "I quite understand."

"I woke up when we stopped and the man opened the gate and the sheep ran out. It was still dark so he never saw me. I stayed on that sheep's back for a coupla hours, and then, wonder of wonders, I saw one of my own kind."

"Who was it?"

"Oh, it was that dear Mrs McBustum."

"Crustum McBustum's mother?" asked Bummus quickly.

"Yays. She was out a-huntin' and she took me back to the cave."

"Dolly, what happened to her?"

Dolly froze, and she blinked at him once or twice. Then she took a great interest in licking a paw and running it over her face. "We-all don't speak about that," she said eventually. She sighed yet again. "How I do miss my lady-pet," she said. "Do you like Country music?"

"I'm not sure I've ever heard it."

Too late he realized what he'd said.

"Why, I have studied the way she sings and I would be delighted to show you…"

"Ah, please don't bother…"

But it was too late.

"It's no bother. No bother at all."

Bummus stood rooted to the spot as she opened her mouth.

He had never heard anything quite like Dolly's voice. The nearest thing, in his experience, was the loose fan-belt on man-pet's car, combined with the quality of a knife dragged across a chip in a china plate. It was all he could do to keep from screaming.

She was taking a deep breath, and Bummus was bracing himself for what was coming next, when a voice somewhere in the cave behind them shouted huskily:

"Anyone at home?" Then, "Whaddaya know? It's a pussycat penthouse!"

Dolly stopped in mid breath, blinked her big blue eyes, and hurried out.

Chapter 6

Jake the Rake's tale

Bummus shook his head to clear it, then licked his paws and passed them repeatedly over his ears. When his hearing had returned to something like normal he wandered out into the cave to see what was happening. Dolly had joined a small group who'd been inside while it was raining and had now gathered around the newcomer. Bummus noticed that the three kittens were among them. A stocky black cat with a white flash down his nose was standing there confidently. He had a white hat with a narrow brim, which he wore at a jaunty angle.

"Swell place you got here," he said, looking around. "Not bad. Not bad, at all."

Dolly seemed quite enamoured. She fluttered her eyelashes and said, "By any chance would y'all be from New York?"

"Well I'll be… a Southern belle, here in Scotland! And a real looker at that! Hey, you know the Big Apple, then, baby?"

Dolly got up. Her fur seemed to expand all over, and her tail rose vertically as she minced forward.

"My lady-pet did a concert there," she said. "That's how I recognized your accent. I have a very musical ear," she added modestly.

"That's nice. Me, I'm tone deaf totally. What do they call you, babe?"

"I'm Dolly Sparkle," she said.

"A pleasure. My friends call me Jake the Rake."

"What do your enemies call you?" Crustum said, looking up at him curiously.

"Huh, I ain't saying. I never use bad language in front of a lady. E-specially," he added, giving Dolly a winning smile, "a lady as peachy-lookin' as this one."

Dolly fluttered her eyelashes again.

Gladys Morningbags said, "Are you hungry?"

"T'anks, but I ate on the way. Rabbit. Not bad."

"Where did you come from?" Bummus asked.

"Flew out of La Guardia."

Bummus blinked.

"Flew? How?"

"You didn't notice the wings? Whassamatter with you, you dumb or somethin'? In a plane, of course."

Gladys said, "Do you want to sit by the fire and tell us about it?"

"Sure, why not?"

They gathered around the fire. Bummus noticed that Dolly was careful to get a place next to Jake. Jake sat, then stood, then sat again. He seemed filled with restless energy.

"See, I'm walking down 130th Street from Fifth when a guy comes out of a big black limo and crosses the sidewalk. He goes up to this house, rings the bell and steps back. At this moment someone tries to drop a piano on him. Now I don't know why I'm looking up, but I am, and I see it coming. So I give a yell and scram so fast I knock his legs out from under him and because of that the piano misses him by inches. He's sitting there on the sidewalk and he reaches his hand inside his jacket and he pulls out a piece and blam! blam! he's blasting away at someone up at the third floor window.

Then this body comes floatin' down and hits the deck. By now the sidewalk's getting kind of crowded, what with this wrecked piano and the body an' all. The guy puts the piece away, looks at me, and says, 'Whaddayaknow? This bag of fur saves my life!' Then he says, 'Jump in the car', so I do."

Jake extended a paw towards the fire and wiggled his digits.

"Turns out this guy is none other than Tony Capelli. Very big with the mob. Has a nasty temper and makes a lot of enemies – hence the piano. But he is very superstitious, and he says I bring him luck, and now nothing will do but I have to go everywhere with him.

"Anyway, he is flying to Glasgow with some other high-rollers for a big pow-wow with the local *padrones*. It's a private plane, so I go with. This is my first time in a plane, and to tell you the truth I am not crazy about it. Well, we're coming to the end of the flight and at this point the pilot says the weather is not looking too good in Glasgow and he has to land at Prestwick. Then Capelli gets into an argument with Rudy Santini and a fight breaks out. It seems this disagreement is more serious than usual because they open the door and toss him out. Then they throw me out too, which I consider a very unkind thing to do, as they have no beef with me."

"You fell out of a plane?" Crustum said.

"Yeah, not too far, though, because the plane is coming in to land. I think it doesn't do much for Tony Capelli, but me, I land in a haystack."

"That was lucky."

"What can I say? I'm a lucky kind of a guy." He shot a smile at Dolly. "I figured I'd head down to Glasgow."

"There's a lot of water in Glasgow," Bummus warned.

"Here, too? You know, they built this big wall round New York City, but no one can say how long it's gonna last. Still, the way I see it, if the families were planning a meet in Glasgow, there must be some dry spots around."

"You can stay with us, if you like," said Gladys.

"Thanks, but the countryside don't agree with me. Gives me hay fever – forget-about-it. I like the city. Well," he got up. "I must be getting along."

Dolly wilted in evident disappointment. Jake looked at her.

"You know, a smart chick like you is wasted hanging out up here in a cave. The city's where it's happening, babe."

"I do miss show business so," she said.

"Why don't you tag along? We can hit the highlights, you and me."

Dolly looked up at him, then round at us. "Well, I declare," she cooed. "I do believe you have persuaded me."

She got up and they walked over to the cave entrance together.

Bummus heard her say, "I can sing on the way."

"Makes no difference to me, kiddo. Like I say, I have tin ears."

Everyone came outside to watch them go. Just before they disappeared down the hill, Dolly turned for the last time.

"'Bye, y'all," she shouted.

"'Bye, Dolly. Good luck."

Bummus looked at Gladys. "Do you think she'll be all right?"

Gladys smiled. "Oh yes. You could say they were made for each other."

Chapter 7

Evel Weevil's tale

As he was outside already and the weather was now fine, Bummus decided to collect some more wood for the fire. He looked around him. Above the cave the moor gained in height until it reached a kind of plateau. There was plenty of gorse and heather up there but he'd noticed that it burned through very quickly when he put it on the fire. What he really needed was a decent chunk of something. It would be heavy but he might be able to drag it back and it would be worth it if it saved him a dozen trips. He set off to explore the hillside further round from the cave.

He hadn't gone far when he saw the frothy green tops of some trees, and before long he was in amongst them. It was hardly a wood, but it was a good stand, and they were not conifers but broad-leaves like the ones he was used to back in London. His paws sank into a soft brown carpet of leaf litter and the air smelt earthy and moist. Some of the trees looked quite old. It seemed like there was a good chance of finding the odd fallen branch.

He began to explore, lolloping over roots and stepping high through the clearings. And then he heard a soft rustling immediately above him. Instinctively he dropped into a crouch and looked up.

At first he could see nothing except the leaves moving gently together or parting to let through a dazzling glimpse of the sun. He waited, ears swivelling, and heard the rustling again. Looking quickly in that direction he saw a furry shape detach itself from the shadows at the base of a bough. It wasn't moving jerkily enough to be a squirrel. He shifted warily, back low, legs doubled, to get a better look. Presently the shape emerged into the dappled light. It was a cat, one he hadn't seen before.

"Hullo," it said.

"Hallo," answered Bummus uncertainly. "Who are you?"

"Who am I?" came the loud and indignant reply. "I am the one-and-only, the world-famous Evel Weevil."

The cat walked boldly along the bough, then nindled carefully along the thinner of two branches, paws well spread, out to the very tip. The branch swayed dangerously and began to bounce up and down. He crouched as it sank, then used the return to make an enormous leap to a mere twig extending from a neighbouring tree. It bent under his weight, and his back legs fell free, but he hung on with his front legs and swung himself up again. Then he teetered to a thicker part, dropped lightly to the branch below, and walked out until he was just above Bummus's head. The sunlight made a halo of his fur and whiskers.

Bummus blinched, then walked to a place where the sun wasn't in his eyes, sat down, and let his tail curl slowly round his paws. The cat, he observed, was similar in size to himself, but his coat was an odd mixture of colours: ginger, white, and black. A patch of ginger and a patch of black started at his ears and met in a line down the middle of his nose, giving him a faintly comic expression. As he stared into the shadows where Bummus was sitting, his pupils expanded until his eyes appeared totally black.

Bummus screwed up his whiskers. "Aren't you coming down?"

"I prefer it up here. I love heights – always did. Down there I'm just another moggy. Up here, I am an artiste!"

He threw up his front paws for emphasis, and the branch wobbled so much he had to regain his balance.

"It looks a bit dangerous to me," Bummus said.

"Ah, but that's what I love – the danger, the adrenaline rush of paws splayed on impossibly thin fences. Not just fences: walls, roofs, telegraph wires – and the higher the better. That's the way to travel. Especially," he added, in a more matter-of-fact tone of voice, "when everything down below is covered in water."

"That's how you got out, then."

"Of course. My paws barely touched the ground."

"I haven't seen you in the cave."

"That's because I stay outside as long as possible. But I do sleep there – on a very high ledge that nobody wants. It's perfect for me. Do you climb trees?"

"Not unless I have to."

"You should try it. Trees are the best of all. A stairway to the sky! You can see for miles, and…" He extended his front paws and hollowed his back. Bummus heard *scritch-scratch, scritch-scratch,* and a light rain of dust and tiny fragments of bark danced and sparkled as it fell through the sunlight. "And," he continued, "you can sharpen your claws anywhere you like without someone shouting at you." He straightened up. "Well, I must go. What did you say your name was?"

"I didn't. It's Bummus. Bummus McBaggus."

"Well, nice talking to you, Bummus McBaggus. Goodbye."

So saying, he clawed up the trunk to an equally thin branch, walked out along it and disappeared from view. Bummus heard a few more crashes in the foliage, then all was quiet again.

He sat there, thinking about the conversation. From time to time he'd shinned up a tree to escape a stupid dog, but he'd never thought of doing it for fun. An idea was forming in his head. As Evel had pointed out, from a tree you get a good view. If there weren't too many leaves in the way perhaps he could spot fallen branches from up there. It would be quicker than searching on the ground. He crossed to the one recently vacated by Evel Weevil, squatted back and jumped up to the first branch, scrabbling the finish quickly with his claws. It really wasn't hard. He went for the next branch and the next, forgetting his original purpose until, more quickly than he realized, he was balancing on a thin branch at the top of the tree, looking out over the landscape.

The tree was a tall one and he could see right to the

horizon. The cave wasn't quite visible from here but he knew roughly where it was. Now he could see that after the moor sloped up to the plateau it dipped into a broad glen. The terrain on the other side was much more rugged, with what looked like a thin covering of grass pierced by great rocky outcrops, and the ground was littered with large boulders. As he looked down at these he caught a glimpse of something moving. Something large.

He waited patiently, wondering if he'd imagined it. As the minutes passed he thought he must have done. Evel Weevil's unexpected entrance had startled him and he was probably still a little jumpy. He was thinking about going down when he saw it again, a dark shape gliding among the rocks. It seemed to be about the right size for a goat, but it didn't move at all like a goat. In fact it moved smoothly, like a cat.

A cat? It can't be – it's far too big for a cat!

He watched and waited, the branch beneath his paws swaying to and fro in a sea of leaves that rustled gently in the wind. Then the shape materialized again and this time he had a clear impression of dark, tabby fur.

It was a cat, all right, but it was huge – much, much bigger even than Håkon, the tabby Norwegian Forest Cat who used to live down the road from him. What had started as mere curiosity now changed, and an awful feeling of dread trickled through him and curdled his stomach with fear.

Could this be what the kittens and Pete and Dolly hadn't wanted to talk about? And was this why the cats never hunted at night and why Pete said to come inside if it was misty? He felt a tingling right down to his paws when he remembered the way he'd wandered around picking up material for the fire without a care in the world – and all the time this... this creature, had been out there! He really had to ask someone about it.

Getting down from the tree turned out to be a good deal more difficult than getting up. He lowered himself, paw by paw, clinging desperately to the bark with his claws. From time to time he paused and went out onto a limb of the tree to size up the situation. The ground always seemed to be a long way off and looking down made him feel quite dizzy. Back at home the obvious thing to do would be to miaow pitifully and wait for someone to rescue him. But he wasn't back at home and there was no one to help him, so he would have to manage as best he could. Eventually he reached a level where the branches finished, turned to face the ground and almost ran down the trunk, leaping out at the last moment. He landed quite heavily but the leaf litter was soft. He took a deep breath and hurried back towards the cave.

He was just thinking about who would be the best

person to ask when he heard some shouting. Ahead of him a kitten was racing down from the plateau. It stopped outside the cave, paused for breath, then shouted in all directions.

"Everyone! Everyone! Baddersley's back!"

Chapter 8

Sir Baddersley Pike's tale

There was quite a stir. Cats ran in from the surrounding area and a few emerged from the cave. Sir Baddersley Pike had returned and it seemed like everyone was turning out to greet him.

"How far away, Ponky Poo?" someone asked the kitten who'd done all the shouting. He looked a good deal older than Crustum, Molly, and Flumbo.

"Just up there, coming down the hill. And he's got something big."

Bummus felt a huge surge of relief. The dark shape he'd seen must have been Baddersley, or whatever it was he was carrying.

A few minutes later the cat appeared, tacking down the moor with something large dangling from his jaws. A whisper went around.

"It's a pheasant."

"No," said Ponky Poo, who was standing next to Bummus, lifting his nose to snurf repeatedly at the air. "It's a capercaillie."

Bummus snurfed as well, but all he could detect was a strangely objectionable smell, and it was coming from Ponky Poo. Pete Gumbo came over to join him. Pete stood, Bummus noticed, on the opposite side to Ponky.

"It's a capercaillie, right enough," Pete said, pausing to lick a paw and pass it over his whiskers. "If I'd known that little lot was coming, I wouldn't have ruined my appetite."

The crowd parted to make way for Baddersley, who trotted right to the front of the cave and set down his prize.

Bummus had never seen a capercaillie before and his attention was divided between that and the fine specimen of a cat who'd delivered it. Baddersley was a large Blue British Shorthair, with orange eyes and quite the most superb set of drooping moustache whiskers Bummus had ever seen. The bird was the size of a chicken, and Bummus could only imagine the strength and determination it had taken to catch something like that and carry it over the hills. No wonder Baddersley was held in such high esteem.

On the other hand, he thought, with a return of his unease, there wasn't the remotest chance that Baddersley, with or without his catch, had been what he'd seen from the tree.

By this time Lady Pike had appeared and she was passing swiftly back and forth along her partner. They nuzzled each other in greeting. The twins were not far behind, and tried to climb up his legs.

"Oo, Daddy, you're so clever!" cried Poppy.

"It's huge, Pop! How on earth did you get it?" Mungo asked.

Baddersley bent down and gave each small head an affectionate lick. Then he spoke in a rich voice, loud enough for everyone to hear.

"Came across this bird at the foot of the Old Man of the Mountains," he said.

Bummus looked enquiringly at Pete, who raised his eyes to the sky, then shook his head. "Must be three miles north of here, man. He's only dragged it all that way."

"Collared the blighter coming through the

heather," Baddersley continued. "Put up the devil of a fight, I can tell you, but I knew I had him. Keep us going for a bit, what?"

His audience cheered lustily, then took it in turns to go up and offer their congratulations.

Pete said, "Come on," and took Bummus with him.

"This here's Bummus McBaggus, governor," he said, nodding in Bummus's direction. "He's just joined us."

"I see, I see. Come far, have you?"

Bummus inclined his head in what he hoped was a suitably respectful greeting. "From London, sir."

"Any hunting down there?"

"Er, there isn't a lot of game round Hendon, actually, but I'd like to learn. I'm good at dodging cars, so I've got quick reflexes and I can think fast."

"Jolly good, jolly good, that's the ticket! Well, we'll soon see what you're made of. We'll be taking out a hunting party when this bird's finished. You can tag along. That suit you?"

"Thank you very much, sir."

As they walked away, Pete said, "You're in luck, mate. He usually hunts alone. Only takes a party out once in a blue moon. Should be wicked."

"Why does he speak in that funny way?"

"Him and his good lady looked after Lord and Lady Longstop. Big place in Berkshire. I s'pose they talked like that and he picked it up."

"How did he end up in Scotland?"

"No idea. He never says nuffin' about that. Septimus might give you a steer. He's known him longer'n any of us."

Septimus! He would be the best person to ask about what he'd seen! Bummus looked around but the elderly cat wasn't in the crowd so he went back into the cave to find him.

Septimus was beating deftly at one ear with his hind paw when Bummus approached. He looked round.

"Hallo there. Baddersley's back, I hear."

"Yes, he's brought a capercaillie."

"Ah, first class."

"Have you known him long, Mr Dufax?"

"Yes, yes, we're old friends. He started this whole thing, you know."

Bummus waited, as it seemed there would be more. Septimus looked dreamily up at the distant cave ceiling as if his memory had been carved there. Then he went on:

"Baddersley's people had a hunting lodge up here in the Highlands. Lady Longstop didn't like to be separated from the cats so they all came, for weeks at a time. It was excellent hunting for them, and I believe Lord and Lady Longstop quite enjoyed themselves, too. Then one day they got word there was serious flooding down south and they hurried back to Berkshire. They left the cats at the cottage. I suppose they thought they'd only be gone for a few days, but they never returned. After a bit, Baddersley got bored with things at the cottage and the two of them struck out across the countryside. They smelt cooking and it led them to this cave. The human was here at that time."

"And when he didn't come back they took the cave over?"

"Yes. More selfish animals would have defended it and stopped others moving in. Not them. They're big on charity, the Pikes. Welcomed any cats who stopped by and shared whatever they had. Smellysox and Crompton and I were among the first. After that I suppose word just spread. Now we're a sizeable community. Most cats are solitary. We've learned to work together. Strength in numbers, you know."

Bummus nodded. He was anxious to turn the conversation.

"Mr Dufax, I climbed a tree when I was out this afternoon and I saw something on the far side of the glen. It looked like a tabby but it couldn't have been any ordinary cat – it was far too large."

Septimus Dufax's round amber eyes widened. "Are you sure?" His voice was a whisper.

Despite himself, Bummus found he was responding in a whisper. "Yes, quite sure. It was big and dark and it was moving smoothly amongst the boulders. What was it?"

Septimus appeared to be turning something over in his mind. Finally he leaned towards Bummus.

"Don't breathe a word of this to anyone. The little ones would have nightmares for weeks if they heard about it. As for the others – well, they get very uncomfortable at the very mention of..."

"Of what, Mr. Dufax? You must tell me!"

"The Claw."

"The Claw?"

"There's a legend round here of an enormous Wild Cat. It comes out of the mist and kills anything that moves. Then it disappears, leaving not a trace behind."

Bummus's mouth had gone dry.

"Did it take Crustum and Molly's mother. And Flumbo's, too?"

"We can't be sure. They just disappeared. They were big, though, too big and strong to be taken by a buzzard. An eagle, perhaps, but we've never seen one here. When we came back from our search, Gloomie McDoom told us the legend of The Claw."

"Why do they call it that?"

"They say it has only one claw on the left front

paw, but it's as large as a scythe."

Bummus nodded grimly. "So that's why no one hunts at night! But this thing was around during the day. Someone should have said something."

Septimus sighed. "I suppose I'm as guilty as the rest. We think that if we don't talk about a problem, it will go away. But then, we're only feline."

"Well, at least now I know I have to look out for it."

"Yes. But listen, Bummus: if you should see it, *run for your very life!*"

Chapter 9

Sergei Whiskersoff's tale

They lost no time in starting to pluck the capercaillie. The kittens joined in the fun, chasing the floating feathers and jumping up to bat them.

Bummus sat down and watched them from inside the cave entrance for a moment. Like all cats he knew better than to hurry anywhere without pausing for a good think. It struck him that the fire must be getting low. He'd gone outside to find more fuel but in the fear and excitement of seeing that enormous cat he'd come back with his jaws empty.

He rose to go out again but just as he was stretching his front legs Pete came towards him accompanied by a strange-looking cat.

"'Ere, Bummus. Thought you'd like to meet Sergei."

They greeted each other.

"The pleasure is mine," said Sergei, pronouncing the 'p' of 'pleasure' so hard that a tiny bit of spit landed on Bummus's cheek.

"Let's go inside," Pete said, and they walked back into the cave.

Bummus looked over his new acquaintance.

"Are you Russian, Sergei?"

"Not Russian, Siamese. But my womansk is Russian prima ballerina with Royal Ballet. Very highly strung, my womansk. Especially when she is reading reviews of performance in paper. Is taking only one bad comment and completely she fly into rage. Worse than this is no comment at all."

Pete guffawed. "I've known a few chicks like that."

"It take a lot to calm her down," Sergei continued. "I

do a few moves, you know, the dainty trot around room, the neat leap to very high shelf or back of armchair. And she say, 'Oh, Sergei, if I could leap through the air like you, everyone say I am the finest dancer in the whole world.' Then I jump on her lap and she stroke me so hard my rump go way down and then way up high. Crazy womansk."

He grinned.

Bummus noticed that the others were coming back into the cave, several of them dragging the half-plucked capercaillie. Drops of water clung to their fur. They shook themselves and settled down to some serious licking.

He turned back to Sergei. "I like your coat. It's so sleek and short."

"Yes, would find hard to cope with lot of hair."

"Bit chilly for up here, though, I would have thought," Pete said.

"A little, maybe. But..." he leaned forward with a conspiratorial whisper. "I show you."

He crossed the cave prettily and without a break in his stride flowed through the air to the ledge to join Count Gropius. Sergei mooched the Count's face and nuzzled his ears.

The Count was delighted. "He's so affectionate, the dear. Isn't he affectionate?"

Sergei settled down next to him, completely covered by the Count's long white coat. Then he peered out at them from under the fur with a knowing look in those slightly crossed blue eyes.

"What it is to have friends, eh?" Pete murmured to Bummus.

Presently Sergei got up.

"Going so soon?" the Count said.

"Back later," Sergei replied, giving the Count's ear a lick. Then he jumped down and rejoined the others.

"You see?" he said.

Bummus nodded. "You're a survivor, all right, Sergei."

"Exactly. The world ends, I will survived."

"Tell Bummus how you got out, Sergei."

"Hah, when Royal Ballet is flooded, my womansk she pack her bags and put me in basket and we go to station. I am looking out of holes in basket. Train is full, this I can see. Every people is crowding into carriage, sitting on floor, standing in aisle. My womansk she go absolutely completely off head. She is scream she has First Class ticket and she is shout for guard until someone tell her to shut it up. Whole journey she is sobbing – is getting on my nerves. At Glasgow I do the very big miaowing, and she open basket to see what is problem. I make the leap and run like crazy. I am pussycat. Like you say, I know to survive. Humans not."

"Do you miss her?"

"A little. Most of all I miss ballet. I do a little dancing myself, you know, in wings. Copy dancers on stage."

Pete Gumbo looked interested. "Go on, then, Sergei. Give us a twirl."

The ones who'd just come in sat down expectantly.

"Well, it is long time, and I am out of practice…"

"Go on, Sergei, old fruit," Pete insisted. "Don't be shy."

"Very well."

He composed himself, ran across the cave floor, did several fine leaps, and twiddled all his legs in the air. There was a scatter of enthusiastic applause. He strode back, smiling modestly, and gave his silky coat a lick.

"That was wonderful, Sergei," said Bummus.

"Awesome," agreed Pete.

"You like?" he said, flashing his blue eyes. "I show you my speciality."

Again he prepared himself, then with a quick pirouette he began a series of leaping turns, one after the other, in a great circle around the cave. Everyone murmured in excitement, but Bummus had seen something the others hadn't.

"The fire, Sergei! Watch out for the fire!"

But it was too late. Sergei's whirling progress took him straight through the fire, scattering twigs and glowing embers in every direction.

"Ai-yai-yai-yai-yai-yai!" Sergei shouted, hopping around holding one paw and then another.

Pete ran over to him. "You all right, Sergei? Here y'are, give 'em a good lick."

"Pete!" Bummus shouted. "Oh my goodness, just look at the fire! Quick, everyone gather up the pieces!"

They tried to help but anything that was burning was far too hot to handle and the rest was just ashes and black embers.

"There's a bit of a glow left," Pete said, surveying the remains. "It might be okay if we feed it. Where's the dry stuff?"

Bummus felt his stomach go down. There was no dry stuff, because he hadn't brought any in. He raced to the entrance.

It was pouring with rain.

Chapter 10

Bummus in disgrace

"I say, this is a bad business, Bummus McBaggus – a very bad business."

Bummus hung his head as he crouched in front of Sir Baddersley. All the other cats had assembled in the cave, and were looking on.

Gloomie McDoom moaned, "It'll be mighty cold come the winter, mighty cold. We'll nae survive another year."

Count Gropius Crudnitz shouted "Banish him!" and some others joined in the chorus:

"Banish him! Banish him!"

Baddersley jerked his head in their direction. "You hear what they're saying? You were in charge of the fire and the fire's gone out. They want you to be banished. What d'ye think of that, then. Hey?"

Bummus couldn't look him in the eye. "I don't deserve any better," he said morosely.

Pete intervened. "Here, governor, it wasn't all the little mogbag's fault. I was egging on Sergei to strut his stuff, and it was Sergei who went through the fire."

"Banish them all!" shouted Count Gropius.

Baddersley looked hard at the Count. "Count

Gropius, I believe you have a liking for rabbit." He left a short silence. Everyone knew that the Count loved rabbit. "May I ask when the last time was that *you* caught a rabbit?"

All eyes turned curiously to the Count. He was flustered. "Er, er..."

"Quite. Whereas Pete Gumbo here catches several a week – which you no doubt enjoy. And you want to banish him, do you? As well as your great friend Sergei?"

Sergei was looking cross-eyed daggers at the Count.

The Count slipped his head to one side. "Ah, I didn't mean permanently..."

Baddersley turned away from him.

"Well now, out there a chap probably wouldn't survive for long on his own. I wouldn't like to do that to Pete or Sergei, or even poor old Bummus here. But there has to be some punishment. Bummus, when the hunting party goes out in a day or two I've decided you will not be joining us. Do you understand?"

"Yes, sir."

Bummus felt a pang of disappointment at being left out of something he'd been looking forward to so much. On the other hand it was a great relief that he wouldn't be ejected from the community entirely.

The meeting broke up, with a lot of grumbling as people went back to their favourite nooks. Sergei, hobbling a little, turned his back pointedly on the Count and went to curl up next to Olga Shagpile, a brown tabby Siberian with white paws and an enormous white ruff.

Bummus remained behind, still looking at the floor. He heard a gentle voice next to him.

"You mustn't feel badly about it, Bummus. I saw what happened. It wasn't your fault, was it?"

He looked round. It was Rhonda Flame. He'd seen her before but only from a distance. She sat softly at his side and regarded him out of solemn copper eyes. All he knew about Rhonda was that she came from Cardiff, and she was a Red Somali. She was not dazzling like Dolly, but she was fine and elegant, and – unlike Dolly – she had a low, melodious voice. But she was a top pedigree, and a great friend of Lady Pike, whereas he was a plain old black-and-white moggy, and he was in disgrace. The social gulf between them was so huge that he didn't even feel awkward talking to her.

"You're very kind, Rhonda, but I know I've let everyone down."

"You took all the blame – for Pete and Sergei, too. That was noble of you. I'm sorry you won't be going on the hunt."

He shrugged. "That's the way it is. I don't suppose
Sergei was planning to go anyway, but I wouldn't have
wanted Pete to miss it."

He sensed her movement rather than heard
anything. When he glanced in her direction she was
standing.

"This is hard after all you've endu-wered to get here,
Bummus. But there is good in you. I feel it. Things will

get better. You just have to believe in yourself."

He shook his head.

"All I want to do is get the fire back. I've piled up dry stuff all ready in the corner."

She tilted her head.

"Ah, but it's going to be hard for a cat to light it, now, isn't it?"

*

To be left out of the hunting party was bad enough, but some of the cats seemed to think it wasn't sufficient punishment. After the incident they avoided him. Even the kittens seemed reluctant to spend much time in his company. He would pass the day outside on the moor just above the cave. When it rained he stayed there, as motionless as a statue, letting the rain soak his fur and drop off his whiskers. At night he would give himself a shake and slink in near to the entrance of the cave, a place that no one wanted, and shiver himself to sleep.

*

Three days later, as soon as the sun was up, the hunting party assembled. Bummus watched from his perch above the cave as they came out: Mrs Tibbs, Gladys Morningbags, Pete Gumbo, Kypo McDonagle, Olga Shagpile, Meatball McPickles, Flashpad McGraw. Even the Count presented himself – probably, Bummus thought, because he'd been shamed into it.

Crummus and Molly raced out to join them, but

Flumbo trailed a little.

"Come on, Flumbo!" Crummus shouted. "They're letting us go with!"

"How far is it?"

"How far? I'm not sure. Would you like me to ask Sir Baddersley exactly where he's left a pheasant or a curlew for us to find?"

"Come on, Flumbo," said Molly. "Maybe a long walk will help with those 'big bones' of yours."

Lady Pike came out with Rhonda Flame to wave them off. He felt a little tug in his chest as Rhonda sat down with an imperious sweep of her magnificent tail. It was clear that they would not be accompanying the party, but the twins were jumping up and down in front of Baddersley in great excitement.

"Please, Dad," Mungo pleaded. "It's a lovely day. Do let us come with."

"It would be just too awful to be left behind," cried Poppy.

Baddersley looked at Lady Pike. "They're big enough now, dear. And it's time they learned a bit about hunting. What do you think?"

She sighed. "All right. But," she said to the twins, "you be good. Stay close to your father. No wandering off, no complaining, and definitely no asking to be carried."

The twins were too overjoyed to reply. Lady Pike

exchanged a despairing glance with her partner and she and Rhonda walked back into the cave.

Chapter 11

The hunt

Baddersley led them up the hill, over the plateau, and down into the glen. A rabbit went sprinting and pronking away through the heather and the kittens looked expectantly at the older cats but they were not to be distracted. The party walked on, climbed out of the glen, up through the rugged landscape on the other side, and down onto a slope that ran below the mountains. The path here was stony, and little grew except thin grasses, mosses, liverworts, and the orange, white, and black lichens that covered the older rocks. In one or two places, small streams emerged, apparently from nowhere, and trickled down the hillside. Where they flowed the grass was bright green, and plants with tiny blue, mauve, or yellow flowers peeped out from the moist pockets between the rocks. Otherwise the terrain was very bare and the ground was hard and hot under their paws.

Flumbo began to moan a little but he received little sympathy from Crummus and Molly. The twins, Mungo and Poppy, hadn't said anything for a long time, and they were walking slowly with their heads low. An area of moorland appeared ahead. Baddersley lifted his head and snurfed.

"Partridge," he said. "Probably a flock of them. Stay here."

He went a little higher up the mountain to get a better view. He watched for some time, flicking the tip of his tail gently. Then he returned.

"Right," he said. "They're hard to spot if they keep still but the silly blighters will move if something disturbs them. Count, you're good and visible. Go up there to the top of the heath. Walk along behind the ridge, then come down through the centre."

The Count looked in utter dismay at the prickly expanse of heather and bracken and opened his mouth, then closed it. He swallowed and started off up the hill. They watched him until his white britches waggled out of sight.

"Right. Crummus, Molly, Flumbo – you stay here with the twins. You can watch what happens but I don't want you under my paws. Pete, Mrs Tibbs, Flashpad – with me. The rest of you, fan out below. If they run, pounce. If they start to fly, jump and try to swat them. Let's give it our best shot now."

He led the way in hunting posture, legs folded so much that his elbows peeped higher than his shoulder-blades, barely visible among the clumps of heather. Pete and Mrs Tibbs followed close behind; like him, they travelled low.

Everyone else got into position and waited. Then a large white ball of fur started to come towards them. It was Count Gropius, trotting angrily down, wincing and cursing at everything that caught on his fur or pricked his pads. Immediately there was a great stirring in the heather. Partridges detached themselves from cover and began to run. Some took off with a great rattle of wings and the air was full of commotion. Cats pounced and jumped, birds clacked and flapped, and feathers flew. Crustum, excited by the action, pounced on Flumbo's tail, and soon all five kittens were wrestling and rolling over one another. By the time they'd paused to look up it was all over.

Baddersley put down the bird he was carrying so that he could speak. "Muster over here," he called. Then he picked up the limp partridge and trotted off. The Count arrived last, trying to gnash some heather twigs out of his fur and complaining bitterly under his breath.

"All right," Baddersley said. He stopped and surveyed the party. Everyone was panting with exertion and glowing with excitement. "Let's see what kind of bag we've got. Mrs Tibbs, yes. Pete, jolly good. Kypo, excellent. Meatball, good man. Olga! – you've done well. Six birds, not bad, not bad at all."

He looked at the sky.

"The weather's holding. We'll carry this lot back

right away. Take it in turns if you're having problems carrying. No shame in that; it's hard to breathe with a big bird in your mouth. All right? Off we go, then."

*

With so many of the others out on the hunting party the cave was quiet. Bummus spent several hours collecting more dry heather and gorse and some thicker branches, and piling it all up neatly in one corner. Then he tidied up the stones where the old fire had been and put some of the dry stuff in the middle. When at last he'd finished he sat down for a long time, looking at it and thinking. They would probably laugh at him but at least it was ready. All he needed was some way of setting light to it but he simply couldn't think of one. He sighed, got up and went to sit in his usual place on the moor above the cave to wait for the others to come back.

He didn't have long to wait. Soon the air was full of excited shouts. Below him there was a stir as those who had remained behind turned out to see what was happening.

Soon Sergei, Smellysox, Crompton, Septimus – even Gloomie McDoom – were waiting outside. A ragged cheer went up when they saw the fine birds six of the successful party were carrying. The cats mingled outside the cave, weaving in and out, and making a good deal of noise.

Bummus watched, head held low, thinking sadly about all the fun he'd missed, and the lessons in hunting he could have received at the hands of a master like Baddersley.

Then Lady Pike emerged from the cave. She said something and the general commotion faded. She said it again, and now there was dead silence.

"Where are the twins?"

Chapter 12

The Encounter

Bummus stood up, suddenly alert. Everyone was looking around them.

"Great Heavens!" said Baddersley. "Aren't they here? Where the devil...?"

"When did you last see them?" Lady Pike asked, her voice tight with tension.

"We were with them while they ambushed the partridges, ma'am," said Crummus. "We were playing together all the time."

"I told them to stay close when we set off on the return journey," Mrs Tibbs said. She was still breathing heavily. "After that I had my mind on carrying my bird."

"We'll have to go back," Baddersley said. "Look, everyone, I know it's been a long day. I'm going anyway. Anyone who's still got the energy, come with me." Mrs Tibbs stood up. "Not you, Mrs Tibbs. Thank you, but I know how tired you are. Anyone else?"

Six cats stepped forward, and on a nod from Baddersley they set off up the hillside again. Of the original party, only Mrs Tibbs and the Count remained behind.

Bummus raced down off the moor and caught up with Pete Gumbo.

"Pete," he said. "I've got to come with you."

Pete looked round in surprise. "Sure, no problem."

*

They travelled for an hour, back along the path of the return journey, looking in every direction, and stopping now and then to listen. Then Bummus said, "Pete, stop here a moment."

Pete looked at the retreating search party and back at him.

"Let them go," Bummus said.

"Whassamatter? You run out of steam?"

"No, but what they're doing is pointless."

Pete sat down.

"Whaddaya mean, pointless?"

"Look, we know the twins were with the party when you set off for home. If they were tired they wouldn't just plop down. They'd have said something, wouldn't they?"

"Yes…"

"So the chances are they fell back and strayed off the path."

"Right," Pete said, "but they didn't shout or we'd have heard them."

"Then they must have had a good reason for staying quiet."

Pete looked at Bummus. He wiped his pink tongue nervously over his whiskers, first along one side, then along the other. "You think they were being stalked by... something?"

"It's more than likely. And if they were trying to avoid it they could have gone some distance. Just retracing the path isn't going to find them."

"We've got to do *something*, mate."

Bummus thought for a moment. "If you were being stalked, would you go down or up?"

"Well, up there you could be spotted a mile off, so that's no help at all. Down? Well, that's better, there's more cover. But you can't go far before you hit the cliff."

"Cliff?"

"Yeah, there's a drop-off down there. Runs more or less parallel to the route. Hundreds of feet. Hell's bells, you don't think they fell down, do you?"

"Pete, I don't know, but I do think we're wasting our time up here. We should be following that cliff edge."

Pete got up and his tail rose vertically behind him.

"All right. I know where to go. I'll lead the way."

*

They made steady progress, looking all around them and even crouching to peer over the edge of the cliff that always lay to their left. Bummus, who didn't have Evel Weevil's head for heights, contemplated the sickening drop, littered with boulders, and it made his head spin. Any animal that fell down there would have no chance at all. They pressed on.

Suddenly Pete stopped, ears swivelling.

"What was that?"

Bummus listened intently. He could hear a gentle breeze sighing along the cliff edge, the intermittent buzz of insects feeding on heather and gorse flowers, and—

He looked at Pete. "I thought I heard a faint mew."

"That's what I heard." He jerked his head. "It came from up there."

Pete hurried forward, only to stop abruptly. The ground had fallen away here, leaving a yawning gap in front of them. Looking across it they could see the rim on the opposite side. Below it, a sapling was growing out of the sheer rock face. Below that, there was nothing but hundreds of feet of empty air.

Pete turned to the right to skirt around the gap and Bummus followed. They were walking on a dusty slope, almost bare of vegetation and littered with rocks, large and small. A few moments later the opposite side of the cliff came into view again.

Bummus turned his ears forward. The mewing seemed to be coming from up there. And now he saw something move: a small bundle of brown fur. To its right was something grey.

Pete had seen it, too. "It's them!"

He started forward but Bummus caught at him. Something was wrong. Why were the twins huddled together at the very edge like that? He looked round slowly, then nodded up the hill.

Coming slowly down the slope towards the twins was an enormous beast with a dark, tabby coat.

*

Lady Pike was quivering with the sheer effort of staying in control. Rhonda had taken her into the cave.

"You mustn't worry, dear," said Rhonda. "They were probably tired and sat down for a rest."

"They may be lost," said Lady Pike, her voice trembling. "They're only kittens."

"There, there. They won't be lost, now, will they? They've got their eyes and noses."

"Mungo's very good," agreed Lady Pike, her voice rising. "He's got his father's nose…"

This finally broke the dam holding back her grief. She put her face on her paws and her whole body shook.

Outside, Gloomie McDoom had his own version of the prospects.

"They'll nae find a trace of 'em now," he said darkly. "They'll have been snatched by a buzzard, or taken by you-know-what."

Septimus stiffened and his tone was unusually sharp.

"You just take your big black cloud somewhere else, Gloomie McDoom. Lady P is quite upset enough without your pessimistic prognostications."

*

Pete froze as he followed Bummus's gaze. "Oh my ears, it's The Claw! I'm off!"

"You can't run now, Pete."

"Can't I? Just watch me."

Bummus took a deep breath and let it out shakily.

"Go on then," he said. "I'll deal with this myself."

"Are you bonkers?"

"What do you want to do? Go back to the others and say we saw the twins, and either they fell over the cliff or they were eaten by The Claw but we didn't hang around to find out?"

Pete swallowed. "Look, mate, I can be handy in the odd scrap, but I know me limits. I'm no match for that brute. Look at the size of it! It's not even flesh and blood – they say it's some sort of phantom that rises out of the mist on the mountains." He was quaking.

"It looks real enough to me. I'll tell you what. There's a patch of gorse on the hillside up there. Make for that. Stay out of sight, but watch what happens. You'll have a good view from there and I may need you."

"What are you going to do?"

Bummus shivered, then drew himself up.

"I'm going to draw him off."

Chapter 13

The Claw

Only a lizard could have travelled lower than Pete Gumbo as he crept up the slope, using every rock, every blade of grass for cover.

He was still trembling from the sight of that monstrous cat. When finally he reached the patch of gorse he sank behind it with a sigh. His curiosity quickly got the better of him though, and he peered between the branches.

The first thing he saw was The Claw and he ducked down instantly. He gulped, then peeked out again.

Below him, the long, rock-strewn slope stretched down to the cliff edge where Mungo and Poppy crouched, still mewing pitifully.

Closer to him —still far too close for his liking – the dark hindquarters of the big cat changed shape rhythmically as it advanced slowly on the two kittens, spreading one giant paw after the other on the dusty ground. The only sound it made was a curious tap-tap as that great claw contacted the hard ground. The distance shrank, yard by yard. He could see no sign of Bummus.

Suddenly the huge cat stopped dead and raised its head slightly. Pete looked round and his mouth dropped open. Bummus had emerged from behind a boulder and he was walking across the open ground in front of the kittens.

Everything went very, very quiet.

*

Bummus's heart was hammering in his chest. Out of the corner of his eye he could see that the animal had halted in its tracks. He braced himself, then sat down and turned to face it. His blood froze. The creature looked big enough from a distance; up close it was enormous. It had paused in mid-stride, back low, ears flat, and lips drawn back in a snarl that wrinkled its nose right up to the eyes and exposed long, yellow teeth.

He waited, trying to control the cold currents of fear that were running through his small body right down into his paws. The Claw remained motionless. It cocked its head a little, then moved it from side to side.

You may be big, Bummus thought, *but I think you could be stupid, or short-sighted, or both. I hope so, because otherwise I have only a few seconds to live.*

There was no point in saying anything to it; wild cats almost certainly spoke a different dialect. Stupid or not, though, there was one language it would understand.

He arched his back, flattened his ears, and emitted the loudest hiss he'd ever managed.

In reply an unearthly growl escaped from those dreadful jaws.

*

Pete cringed. He could see the creature's tail flicking quickly, left, right, left right. Then the rear quarters wiggled, like any other cat preparing to pounce. He could hardly bear to watch.

Run, Bummus! he thought. Run for your life!

Just as it launched its attack Bummus sprang into action and raced for the cliff edge with the cat bounding along behind him. At the very last moment Bummus veered off and Pete's heart leapt into his mouth as he saw what his little friend was up to.

The Claw was big and heavy; on that surface it would be hard for it to stop. Bummus was trying to lead it over the cliff.

*

Bummus glanced over his shoulder. To his horror the Claw had managed to turn and was still behind him, gaining ground with every huge stride. He'd misjudged it: the big cat was faster and more agile than he'd thought. He scuttled frantically around a large boulder, the ground slipping away from under his paws. The Claw skidded after him, even closer than before. Bummus pushed himself to the limit, extending his legs and stretching his back as he dodged from one side to the other, trying desperately to outrun the animal. He could hear the heavy fall of its paws and the snorting of its breath almost on top of him. The rhythm broke and he ducked as a giant paw swiped over his head. He skipped over some large stones and wrenched himself round to run down the slope. The cliff edge loomed. Again he turned, and again the big cat turned with him. This time Bummus jumped up onto the boulder, but just as he was leaping off on the other side the creature swung a paw and caught him on the flank. The force of the blow sent him flying and he rolled over and over in the dust. Snarling jaws bore down on him and in desperation he twisted away and pelted down the slope. The cliff edge came up again. This time he didn't turn. Instead he launched himself over it and into space.

Bummus had seen the sapling growing out from below the cliff edge and now he made a grab for it with both paws. His weight swung him out and back on the slender stem and he hung there, legs dangling. Before he could draw breath a great shower of stones, rocks and dust exploded from the rim and the sky seemed to darken as a great shape came over – and stopped.

Now the two faced each other, hanging below the edge of the cliff.

Bummus clung to the sapling, swaying over the dizzying drop below. As he'd hoped, his pursuer had seen the danger too late. Unable to stop in its headlong rush it had come over the edge, but managed to twist itself round. It was barely three feet away, suspended from the cliff edge by that one huge claw.

It roared at him, teeth dripping with saliva, eyes red and filled with hatred. The smell of its breath filled the air. Then it swung its free paw. Bummus dodged his head back. He glanced up at the animal's claw. It was supporting a lot of weight.

"Missed!" he taunted.

And for good measure he flattened his ears and hissed defiantly.

Again The Claw swiped but this time there was a popping noise, a blur of dark fur, and suddenly it was no longer in front of him. A prolonged yowl died away, then all was quiet.

Bummus looked down and his head swam. He swayed out again on the sapling and to his horror saw a crack appear in the dusty soil at its base. A trickle of earth and small stones escaped and fell into the void.

The sapling was breaking away.

Chapter 14

Pete to the rescue

"Bummus!"

Pete's black face was peering over the cliff edge, his chops peeled back in a smile of sheer relief. "Blimey, I thought I'd lost you! Hang on, mate." He extended a tentative paw. "No, can't reach you, can you climb up a bit?"

Bummus eyed the bulging soil at the base of the sapling. Even as he looked, another small shower of earth and stones detached itself and dropped past him. He could hear it pattering down the cliff face far below. He was afraid to shift his grip, but he couldn't stay here for much longer. Tentatively he slid one paw up and fastened his claws on the thin trunk. Then he brought up his other paw.

A sudden jerk startled him, and another shower of stones came past. One of the roots had broken free. He gulped, then took a deep breath and moved his paws up again, slowly and carefully, inch by inch. Pete watched from above, mumbling encouraging noises.

As his weight shifted closer to the base of the little tree, its tip rose up, and now it was whipping back and forth above his head. Pete shot out a long black paw and swiped, once, twice, three times, claws scrabbling thin air in an attempt to hook the tip of the sapling. On the next attempt he succeeded and backed off with it, out of sight.

His muffled voice came floating down. "Okay, I've got it, keep coming."

The sapling was now arched over the edge of the cliff. Bummus brought up his hind legs and, gripping the stem with his toes, he worked his way upwards.

His eyes came level with the cliff edge and Bummus saw that Pete had the sapling in his teeth, his paws folded over it, holding it steady. Bummus reached out one paw and fastened his claws in the dusty ground. They slid back; he couldn't get a purchase. Then a stray gust of wind lifted Pete's baseball cap. For one terrifying moment Bummus thought he'd let go of that slender stem to make a grab for it but he didn't. The cap sailed out, and he followed it with his eyes as it went spinning through the air, down and down to the bottom.

He tried again, and this time got just enough traction to pull himself up. Then he did the same with the other paw. Now, pulling with all his might, he got himself over the edge, crawled a little way forward, and collapsed.

Through the mists in his head he became aware of a gentle nudging and high voices. He opened one eye and found he was looking directly into a small brown furry face.

"Uncle Bummus, are you all right?" Mungo asked.

Poppy was peering anxiously at him from behind her brother. "Please get up, Uncle Bummus."

Then he felt a heavier shove from behind.

"Come on," said Pete. "We're still too close to that drop for my liking."

Slowly and carefully, Bummus rose. Mungo looked up at him.

"You are the bravest pussycat in the whole wide world," he said solemnly.

Bummus gave him a friendly lick. "We'd better get you two back," he said. "The others are still looking for you."

He looked at Pete. "Thanks, Pete. Sorry about your cap."

Pete shrugged. "Never mind my cap. I think you just lost eight lives."

They had begun to walk up the slope when Bummus paused. "Hang on a moment," he said. "There's something I forgot." And he turned back towards the cliff edge.

"What on earth are you doing now?" Pete cried.

Bummus stretched himself out near to where the sapling was peeking above the edge and felt around with one paw. Then he drew back and joined the others.

"What did you go back for?" demanded Pete.

"This," said Bummus, and showed him.

It was a huge claw.

Chapter 15

The reunion

When they got back to the path there was no sign of the search party.

"Half a mo'," Pete said. Then he lifted his muzzle to the sky, formed an "O" with his mouth, and let out a prolonged and terrible wail. He took a deep breath and did it again, then looked at the others. "I used to belong to the local fence choir," he said proudly.

The twins tentatively removed their paws from their ears.

"I thought Dolly was loud enough," said Bummus.

"She's loud, but she ain't musical like me," Pete said. "Let's have another shot."

This time Pete's wail was longer and even more penetrating, and even Bummus flinched. Then, as he straightened up, he heard a shout. A large grey cat was coming over the hill and up the path.

"It's Badders," said Pete. "See, I knew it would work."

"Dad!" yelled the twins and ran to meet him.

By the time Baddersley and the rest of the party had joined them, he seemed to have had the entire story from the twins, complete with embellishments of their own. He greeted Bummus and Pete warmly.

"Well done, chaps! Phew, what a relief! Damn fine job, you two!" Then he gave a conspiratorial chuckle. "Now, who's been filling their heads with a lot of nonsense about The Claw?"

The twins jumped up and down. "It *was* The Claw, dad, really it was! He was going to kill us but Bummus killed *him* instead!"

"Now, now, you two, I know you got lost but—"

"It was, it was! Show him, Uncle Bummus!"

Bummus moved to one side and there, lying on the ground, was the giant claw.

Baddersley's jaw went slack. He regarded it with astonishment, looked at Bummus, then back again, and as the full implications rushed in on him tears came into his eyes. Without a word he stepped up to Bummus and gave his ear one long lick, a token of extreme affection and respect.

The last clear patch of sky was darkening as the group set off for home. Bummus and Baddersley were at the front, followed by Pete and the twins, the rest chattering excitedly behind.

*

The welcome back at the cave was ecstatic. They gazed in wonder at the huge claw and the story had to be told and retold. The area outside the cave became a flowing mass of fur of every different colour. Cats went inside and couldn't resist coming out again, tails erect, to weave and rub against each other in celebration. The air was filled with purrs and squeaky little crows of pleasure. Pete made more noise than anyone.

"You never saw anything like it," he shouted, laughing and waving his paws around. "The creature was simply GINORMOUS, and this – this little black-and-white moggy – only goes right up and hisses in its face!"

When Lady Pike had stopped hugging and nuzzling the twins she went over to Bummus, and the others gathered round to listen.

"What a brave one you are, Bummus!" she said. "I'm so grateful I simply don't know how to thank you."

Bummus hardly knew what to say himself. "Um, that's all right, Lady Pike. It's good to see the twins back with you."

She gave him a searching look.

"Bummus McBaggus," she said, shaking her head. Then she raised her voice so that everyone could hear. "You don't seem to realize. You haven't just rescued my twins. You've made history!"

They all cheered. Under the direction of Septimus, they pushed together some rocks and mounted the claw on it as a monument to Bummus's great deed, then surveyed their efforts with undisguised satisfaction.

The evening wore on. There was little light now, for

clouds had covered the moon. Most of the cats had gone inside, but Bummus had sought out his usual place above the cave and he was up there on his own. Rhonda came and sat softly next to him.

"You see, Bummus? I was right, you're a hero. I knew there was greatness in you."

Bummus looked round. In the half-light, Rhonda's lovely copper eyes seemed bigger and more liquid than ever.

"Oh, Rhonda, I'm glad we got the twins back safely, but youngsters like that – and some of the older ones – are going to have a hard time of it this winter."

"Are you still fretting about the fire?"

"Yes, I am."

"It's not as bad as all that, now, is it? We'll—"

She broke off to make some small exploratory movements with her nose, snurfing the air. Then a strange light illuminated the clouds on the horizon and her ears twitched as a rumbling sound rolled across the landscape. "There's a storm on the way. You should come back in the cave."

"You go in, Rhonda. I'll stay up here for a bit. I like to see the lightning."

"Very well."

He watched her go down, waiting until the tip of her magnificent tail disappeared, and his heart ached more than ever.

Soon the rain came, falling in torrents, and the whole landscape hissed in the deluge. Bummus sat patiently through it, jerking his head from time to time when a particularly large drop landed on his ear. Lightning forked from the skies and great claps of thunder fell and echoed around the mountains. It eased off for a while, and it looked as though the storm had passed through. Bummus rose and had a good shake to loosen up his coat, which the rain had plastered to his body. Then a flash of lightning seared through the air and the sound followed it instantly with a jolt that made him flinch. His ears were ringing and for several moments all he could see was the fading image of the flash. Gradually his eyes adjusted to the darkness once more and he became aware of a flickering glow that seemed to come from just around the hill; it was accompanied by a crackling noise. His ears came forward, then he hurried back to the cave.

"Everyone, quick!" he shouted. The lightning's set a tree on fire! This is our chance."

Chapter 16

Fire!

Paws came from under chins and over noses, and several cats unwound from their sleeping positions on the floor to regard him with wide eyes.

"Quickly!" he cried. "Don't just look at me. Get going – all of you! Pick up the polythene sheet and pull it out of the cave."

Evel Weevil was the first to respond, jumping down from his high ledge. Seeing this, the others got up and started to follow instructions. They took hold of the sheet in their teeth and hauled it over their backs.

"Follow me!" Bummus cried, and they dragged the sheet along as he led the way to the small wood. Sure enough, a tree had been split by the lightning, and half of it was in flames. They looked up at it and then at Bummus.

Evel Weevil moved to stand next to him. He had to raise his voice over the spluttering of the fire.

"What's the plan?"

"I'm going up," said Bummus. "See that branch? It's just the right size. It's burned through at this end but the tip's still going. It'll be hot, but if I can jump up and down on it, it may break off."

"You're not going up. I am."

"It's too dangerous."

"Are you kidding? I'll be in my element!"

And without waiting for an answer Evel sprinted over to the tree and shinned up the half that wasn't burning. Then he made his way gingerly across to the other side. Bummus watched carefully, holding his breath.

The wind gusted and a sheet of flame changed direction, sending a cloud of smoke and flying sparks up around the small animal. Bummus heard a cry and a cough. Then the smoke cleared and Evel was still there, edging outwards. There was another shower of sparks as he started to bounce up and down on the branch.

"That's it, keep going!" Bummus shouted.

"All right for you," Evel shouted back. "This is hot."

The branch was flapping more and more, the flames leaping brightly from the tip, and then, with a crumbling noise, it broke away and dropped to the ground. The crowd below cheered, then went silent. It had gone out.

But Bummus hadn't given up; he'd noticed the effect of the wind. He raced forward, picked up the thicker, charred end of the branch in his jaws and waggled it back and forth. The tip glowed, then burst into flame.

Now Pete Gumbo took charge. "Come on, pick up the plastic sheet. Keep the rain off Bummus as he carries it back. That's it, pull hard, keep it nice and tight."

Bummus ducked underneath, the flaming branch still in his mouth and they moved off. Slowly they carried the sheet up the slope towards the cave, straining with their jaws and falling over each other. Bummus's gums were burning from the wood, which was still very hot, but still he refused to let go. Above his head large raindrops pattered loudly and unevenly on the taut sheet. He was dimly aware of Pete running round, yelling encouragement, and he knew his friend would be pulling with his own teeth wherever it was needed. But some of the cats were getting very tired. The plastic sheet sagged and flames licked up from the end of the branch and melted a hole in the sheet. Big drops of rain came through and sizzled on the branch. Now it would be a race against time.

They struggled on and still the rain came in and sizzled, yet the branch continued to burn.

"Keep going," Pete shouted. "We're nearly there!"

Bummus's hopes began to rise. They were going make it! They'd just turned to enter the cave when the wind, coming from a different quarter, blew the flame towards him. A flash of heat washed over his face and singed his whiskers and he cried out, dropping the branch. It landed in a puddle that extinguished it instantly. He lowered his head, raised his rear end, and backed out from under the sheet, defeated, and smarting with pain and disappointment.

Another gust of wind came along and, at the edges of the hole in the sheet, a blue flame came up and spread.

"Quick, get it inside," said Pete, and they all helped to pull it into the cave. Bummus showed them where he'd laid the fire and they pushed the burning plastic into it. Within a couple of minutes it was blazing fiercely. The warmth spread and they settled down, exhausted but happy, the firelight flickering on their faces.

"You all right?" Pete asked.

Bummus gave him a crooked smile, through

blistered lips and wonky whiskers.

"Yes, I'm fine. Everything's fine."

Chapter 17

The tail end

Sir Baddersley Pike declared that from that day on Bummus McBaggus would be his second-in-command. Whenever he went hunting Bummus went with him, and when they settled down by the fire in the evenings Bummus was in the place of honour, next to him. On his other side the lovely Rhonda would snuggle up close.

After a while four new kittens had arrived, one with a red coat, one black-and-white, and two with a curious combination of a red coat with black and white on their tummies. They never tired of hearing how their father faced the Claw, and it seemed that Sir Baddersley never tired of telling them the story.

"Because, kittens, it's a lesson to us all. The Claw was big and ferocious, but he was driven by blind fury and it emptied his mind of everything except hate. Your father may be just an ordinary moggy, but he has courage and intelligence. He faced The Claw bravely and he won the day."

"And that," cried Blanco, the black-and-white kitten, "is why the big claw is outside the cave, and it will be there for ever and ever!"

"But everyone says the waters will go down one day," said Ellen, the kitten with the red coat. "And then we won't have to live up here in a cave any more. And there'll be human-pets to feed us, and nice warm houses to sleep in. Everyone says," she finished softly.

Baddersley sighed. "Yes, Ellen, one day perhaps.

And then this cave, our home for so many years, will be cold and empty."

"The big claw will still be outside, though, won't it?" said Blanco.

"Yes," cried Ellen, "but no one will know what it means – not even humans!"

Baddersley shook his great head.

"The claw isn't important, kittens, it's the story. And that will stay with us wherever we go, now, won't it?"

—THE END—

Printed in Great Britain
by Amazon